Before ABC

STAR

Before

Love

I'm Done

Once Upon a Whisper

Couldn't Do It

Rejection

10 Years

Two Of You

Blur

Help Me

Whispering Secretes

If You Don't Want to Think About It

Hunger

A

A Light Unknown

Falling & Failing

Foolish

Scared Without a Reason

Stop

Temptation

Want

Dream

Lights Out

B

New Chapters Begins Fast

Help

Left Unseen

Winter

12 Little Lies

Fear

Sorry (Sorta)

Half Moon

Manipulation

The Evidence

C

My Toy

Stories

Faking It

Trust

Nothing's The Same

Hurry

H.I.F.R

Sacrifices

Stories End Too

To my younger self who wrote these. I hope you'll heal and be okay. All these pieces are written by a 13–14-year-old Star.

Love

First loves are something you never get over but learn from.
I'm numb, so numb.
I can't feel anything below the neck.
You're leaving me
The thing I fought so much for,
The thing that I resented the most,
You, leaving my side.
Now I can't even cry in your pretty arms.
I'm sitting at home,
Waiting for a text,
A letter,
Something from you.
It hasn't even been 5 damn minutes,
And I'm tired,
From being away from you.
I'm so upset,
And numb,
I can't feel.
I need the light you bring again.
First loves are something you never get over but learn from.
I learned from you,
It was one sided again.
But we did love each other.
I don't want more from you,
I just want you near me again,
Next to me.
Love,
I want it so bad.
I need you so much,

I'm going mad.
I'm numb,
To my feelings,
I want you back.
Please come back.
I'm numb, so numb,
Wrap your body around me once more.
I'm not ready to go yet,
To let go,
Come back.
My love?
You left me.
I'm so upset,
I can't even stand it,
I'm so dumb,
I left,
I want to hold you again,
But I have no regrets.

June 14, 2019, 1:15 PM.

I'm Done

I've recorded your voice over and over again,
How many times will you say you'll never fight anymore,
Never talk anymore,
Don't make me laugh.
I'm crashing because I was told to not mind,
To forget and engrave those words into my chest.
So, my car is riding around the long gray streets at night.
I just want to be right.
My mind goes off at the wrong times,
You think men are only ones hiding their pain,
You're weak to not realize I do it too.
I scream but in my head.
Idiot, you went along with me, and we'll crash.
If you're done with the things they have to say.
Sitting alone in your bedroom and waiting for the shouting to stop.
Pulling us down when we have nothing to weigh down with.
It's like I'm already at the bottom of the ocean.
You idiot, what are you going down there?
What do you think?
Swimming will let you get away from the imaginary weight put on by others.
Let's crash together into the mist of the things we missed.
Grab the keys.
If you think I'm not going fast enough,
Wait until the whole world spins and the tears start to burn in our lungs.
I'm buried beneath the boxes,

The voices promising me to get better.
I'm so dark because I can reach the brightness unless we crash.
Don't mind the stares I get and stars that are still bold enough to light the way.
But what happens when I can no longer see those stars?
When I can't crash because I've done too many times?
When I grow too old,
And don't care.
When I can't just stay away.
It may be just a number but it's what they use to judge my decisions.
My tears and love.
What if I notice the sky isn't black but navy blue?
What if I'm told I'm wrong again?
Am I supposed to step on my accelerator and cry.
To crash and break?
Idiots,
I'm surrounded by selfish people.
Idiots,
I tell you I'm surrounded by people who know so much more than me, but I choose to ignore.
Your beliefs are different from me,
But all those idiots gather around,
Picking up the things that'll make them better than the rest.
That'll help the other,
That'll put them past my seniors,
Idiots,
I'm stupid and surprised by the people who want to change so let me tag along.
I'm crashing because I was told to not mind

To forget and engrave those words into my chest
So, my car is riding around the long gray streets at night
Long gray streets,
That don't end,
Air, my sole purpose
But what is it?
Won't I find an answer?

Once Upon a Whisper

Once upon a whisper,
Once upon a time,
Everything in this world,
Seemed so divine.
Once upon a time,
Once upon a whisper,
I,
Was still,
Circling around,
With so much light,
I couldn't seem so right,
About the fight.
Lay in my eyes.
Lay by my side.
I couldn't see the light,
Besides.
Once upon a whisper,
Once upon a time,
I wanted to see,
Such delight.
I wanted,
And I needed,
But I never had a chance,
I sought to make a change,
But nothing came my way.
One,
Day,
I still stayed.
There staring and wanting,
And trying,
Without a single care.

Without a stare,
With no stars in the sky,
And all in black and white.
Once upon a whisper,
One step on a land,
Once a upon time,
Won't give me a dime.
Once upon a whisper,
One step on my land,
Once upon a time,
I saw black,
And white,
Because once in my life,
Something seemed so right,
Yet nothing seemed so wrong,
That I couldn't hear my mind.
Once,
Upon,
A,
Whisper.
Once upon a time,
I wanted to see,
All the world,
With my own eyes.
It was,
Such,
A,
Divine.

Couldn't Do It
Couldn't do it for the first try,
Couldn't say it.
Couldn't say it for the first time.
Couldn't see it,
Couldn't see it, keep it on now.
Didn't want it,
Didn't want all the scars still spraying.
Wouldn't do it,
Wouldn't do it over again.
Shouldn't say it,
Shouldn't say it all over here now.
You wanted something,
I could never give.
Something I could never find,
Myself,
To live.
You wanted candy,
I gave you sweets.
You said they weren't tasty,
They gave him heats.
You wanted candy,
I gave you sweets.
You said they weren't tasty,
They gave him heats.
Keep your mouth shut.
It isn't over right now.
It's hasn't happened,
The mission given isn't real as of now.
You couldn't do it,
You couldn't say it,
You shouldn't show it.

You shouldn't spray it.

Rejection
I can't stand the way I feel,
It's like I've been eating myself inside.
I don't know what to do anymore,
You mean more to me than myself.
My own body,
If I've eaten and if you're starving.
I'm suffocating because of you.
I just want to blame you so much.
I've been cutting myself lately.
I know you let me down slowly,
But you really asked me if I was okay, right after you apologized.
You were my hope, and I don't want to move on.
You say to have hope, but you just broke it.
Our friendship means more to you,
But my heart is crushed.
And I feel your fear from here ma'am.
You left me irrational, and it's been twice.
You were my first, second and last.
You took my love and didn't read through it like a discarded book.
I feel left outside in the cold rain that runs down my cheeks.
Numbness,
You say you've felt the same way.
Numb,
But I can see your messy hair from here.
I'm so naive because even now I think if you're okay and not of my swelling throat.
It's getting harder to breath,
I'm getting lost again,

I feel left behind again.
We are one,
That one was me,
And you stood on the other side of the road completely blind, smiling and shining as I crumbled.
I want to blame you,
Will you take it?
Take the pain from me?
I said I'd talk to you later, but you know the truth.
I hope,
I wish I could drink but I'm too small.
Our friendship is supposed to be long and strong, and it means so much to you but,
It's getting harder to breath,
I'm getting lost again,
I feel left behind again.
You say you've felt this way before and it breaks me.
I still like you, and it fucks me up,
I don't know what to do anymore.
Do you hear me begging?
I'm on the other line crying my heart out.
I'm shouting but I can still smell our fear from here ma'am.
"No, I'm sorry. I love you as a best friend and I love our friendship more than anything, its strong and long"
Then why is it getting harder to breath?
Completely numb as if isn't happening.
I want you still,
Fucking notice, me, before I rip myself,
Apart over and over again because I can't take this pain.
You say you can never deny your feelings
they'll only make it worst,

And I try to say I started liking you.
I was irrational, you didn't do anything.
I'm hit,
You weren't irrational,
You can't help but to fall for someone, it's your feelings
But You ask me why I like you.
Why do you think?
You just explained it to me but you're still blind to the truth.
I can still hear your fear ma'am.
I feel broken and suffocated,
Don't ask if I'm okay,
Because you already know what you've done.
You cut so deep.
And don't realize.
Can you take my anger in those pretty hands?
All I did was deceive myself so know I know why.
Now I know why,
It's getting harder to breath
And I hate it,
I've become a mess.
Angry and tired and glasses of champagne.
I'm left alone and know where the knives are in the kitchen.
Finally, I get it,
Because of me,
Because I'm too afraid to blame you.

10 Years
"Do you think we'll still be friends in 10 years?"
"Yeah, I think so."
"I'll be dead in ten years...."
"WHAT!?!"
There's a short amount of time,
I can't stay here.
Stay by you,
It's pressuring.
I hate it,
But I'm excited to leave.
Excited to be dead by my late 30's,
Why?
I don't know.
You got 10 years to live.
Well, what do I do?
Why ask me?
I'm wanting to leave today.
Have my first death,
Or just the last.
But you know what's funny?
I'll be dead anyways!
I'll be drowning in the black thick blood soon.
My wings will be covered, and I'll swarm myself with darkness.
I'll be dead.
Just wait a little longer.
My heart's aching,
Because I want to stay.
What's a need?
I live by my wants,
That road me down the path of arrogance,

Such a sad thing.
You've got ten years,
Make em' last.
Ten days remain,
Spend em' wisely.
No more sick days,
Work til' your wings fall fast.
Bad, sad,
Don't feel too miserable.
I'm not special anyways,
Do you think we'll be friends in ten years?
"I'd hope so"
What If I tell you I'd be dead?
"Are you okay?
"How are you sure?"
Just got a feeling.
It's gonna happen.
Brace yourselves,
It's about to hurt.
When the comet comes,
Crash upon,
Bodies,
Dead and alive.
Strangeness fills our lungs.
They fail.
Softly,
Down,
Rumble.
Death.
10.
A short word.
How long do you think it is?

In the snap of my fingers, they fly.
They're gone.
10 years,
Funny to think.
No more breathing,
No more running,
No hugs,
No loving,
Nothing.
You've got ten years,
Make em' last.
Ten days remain,
Spend em' wisely.
No more sick days,
Work til' your wings fall fast.
Burn like the ash,
Sprinkled across the floor.
There's something that confuses you,
It's okay,
Fake your time,
Take your life.
It's okay,
Take some time.
Stay there and contemplate,
It's gonna be all fine.
I'm okay.
I don't know,
I don't know,
What's got you worrying?
There's something you don't know,
But no one's mentioned it.
Why?

You want to know?
Burn the skin,
Peel back the ash.
Bring it to me,
Let me taste.
Crumpled onto my tongue.
Let the flakes pierce your skin.
10 years,
A little time.
My bitch,
My departure,
Just wait,
I got a feeling it's gonna happen.

I Know Something You Don't

I know something you don't,
I have a secrete you don't know.
Do you want to know?
I don't think you would be happy.
It's not a thrilling secrete.
But if you beg...
If you cry out in pain...
If you, suffer yourself,
I can give it to you.
There's something weighing down on my chest and you can't see it.
There's something overshadowing my hurt.
You watched someone else lose themselves,
But I sat right under your nose, dying.
You couldn't even reach me.
My eyes burning,
My head spinning,
What if you woke up and I wasn't alive?
What if you lost me because you failed to notice?
You blame me, accuse me.
Aren't you, my family?
How?
You can't even see me?
You don't know me.
There's something you don't like,
Something you can't even bear to think,
And it happened to me.
As you watched him detained,
I sat there bleeding,
None of you even batted an eye.
My blood pumping down to my feet.

The ground cementing me down.
Swallowing my soul,
Leaving the corpse,
That you dragged along playfully.
You saw me weak,
But told me it wasn't that serious.
You said I was too dark,
Imagine my pain?
If you're hurting right now,
Imagine how I felt?
I was alone.
You didn't help me,
You're not the reason I'm alive.
None of you saved me,
I did,
I was alone.
Is your heart pounding?
Are you crying?
Are you okay?
I ask as you, never had.
Never took a look my way.
I stood right next to you, and you didn't notice.
You should be glad I'm even alive.
I could be rotting six feet under right now,
In peace,
In silence,
You accuse?
What right do you have?
My family?
You couldn't save me.
Does it hurt?
There's 7 of us, and yet I was alone.

How are you my damn family?
How do you love me?
I'm not alive because of you,
I couldn't even turn to you for help.
I hope you hurt.
There's something weighing down on my chest and you can't see it.
There's something overshadowing my hurt.
You watched someone else lose themselves,
But I sat right under your nose, dying.
You couldn't even see it,
It was so obvious.
How could you 6 be so stupid?
There was something you didn't know,
Now that I've said it,
Does it hurt?
How do you feel?
It's so fun,
My body is shaking in fear.
Tears brim my eyes and spill down my cheeks,
My heart has sunken.
The world stopped spinning,
Hold your breath,
You're underwater.
There's no way out.
Do you like this feeling?
Silhouettes stare at you,
People you love most,
They don't help,
Do you like this moment?
Are you okay?
You seem a little pale.

Looking a little stale.
If your heart working?
Your shadow won't stop lurking.
Want me to help?
Stare at me,
What do you see?
You like it?
My breathe has stopped, with each piano key.
More air is drawn out.
Tears stopped flowing,
Choke and struggle in my flood,
Need a hand?
It's not that serious!
Stop whining, pain is only in your mind,
Stop being so immature.
If I died?
Choked?
Woke up breathless, which one of you would cry?
I'll tell you; I'd laugh!
What makes you think you can judge me?
I was 13 and almost took my life mom!
My brothers and sisters, my father,
I was sitting right there.
How come you never noticed I wasn't breathing?
It's amusing, right?
How come you never noticed I wasn't breathing?
It was so obvious.
Nothing in my eyes,
My orbs break loose from crying.
Sleeping every day,
Fighting,
How could you have 5 kids and just favor 1?

What's the point of family if you can't be there for me?
I couldn't even turn to you for help.
For my family, I diss you.
How dare you accuse me?
For my family, I'm not alive because of you.
For my oldest brother,
I hurt, it was serious,
I may be immature but alone I broke. Hurting more than you could ever know.
For my family, thy diss thee.
My broken beats were repaired by me,
I don't need your pity,
How do you feel?
Sure, say I'm mad, but I could care less.
I love you,
I truly do, my family,
But be glad I'm alive.
You could've lost me,
And never known why.
Too busy with a man you could never help drive.

Two of You
Looking into a mirror of endless sunshine,
Possibly,
Life,
There's two of you.
I can't fly,
My wings have shattered.
No longer does the moonlight reach my chambers.
The crevices where I'm thrown out,
Forgotten,
Lifeless,
WHAT THE FUCK IS THIS?
Why must I feel this, why?
When looking,
Endless mirrors within,
Obscure version of I,
Staring back into my eyes.
Black dots,
Speckled red,
How do I get past this?
What must I do to feel again?
Take away all the hurt.
Why the hell did this happen,
The quaint,
OH, THE FUCKING AGONY!
I waned to be safe.
Everything,
The top,
Everything,
Nothing happened,
It all ended,
Splendid sweetness turns bitter.

Bitter silence,
Bloody tonsils go ahead and remove them.
It all swarms,
I can't feel myself shine no more.
As if I've fallen into a heat of endless darkness.
When I look into the mirror,
Why must I stare at four eyes,
Black and brown,
Which ones do I own?
Two of me,
Raise my head.
I'll fall deep,
Pits blur,
Blue, purple, black
Oh, the quaint!
Beauty,
Stray,
From two,
Two of you,
Of me,
Why am I to you?
And me?
Two of you,
Two of me,
Looking up into the sunlight.
Hands up,
The suns out,
Won't fall back.
My hands open,
Reach,
Keep falling,
Sleep for a while.

Two of you,
One hand up,
Two of me,
One hand deep in the ground,
Dirt roads carry us to uncertain destinations.
There's no inside,
No matter,
Thorny bushes.
No where to turn,
Help, do you hear it?
Get ready to gear it.
Outside,
Two of you,
Two of Me.

Blur
The days blend together,
The night bends forever,
It's creeping like the shadows,
I can't seem to waver.
Left and right,
Sideways and down,
Up and twisted.
Blue,
Blur,
Shit.
Is that me?
(Ha ha).
Is that my voice?
Is this *my* sound?
Can I hear the mumble?
Dear raven, can you claw into my skull?
(Switch it)
Dear?
Is that you?
Looking into a mirror?
Again?
What do you think you'll find in there?
Dear,
Please come,
Ravens living in a blur.
The clicking is getting to her,
Time stands still.
HEY!
Are you okay?
Are you scared?
Can you see anything?

Or is it still blurry?
Hey,
You,
Yes, you Star Pluto.

Help Me
I can't breathe,
It's suffocating.
My chest tightens,
Hello?
Is anyone there?
Can anyone help with the mess in my mind?
Mind if I light?
Help me!
Something keeps on chasing me,
It won't let my of legs go.
Mind if I blow smoke?
Would you mind looking into my mind?
Mind shoveling though the fungus,
Walking past my demons?
My stomach hurts,
I curl,
I can't breathe any longer.
The pain comes from my stomach,
and slowly rises like the water levels.
Up to my chin I'm underneath,
Help me!
I can't feel with my fingertips,
It's consuming me.
Don't let it take me,
Would you please?
Could you please?
Say please?
Please,
Please,
I beg.
At least ask me first,

If you want my body,
Take it, but please,
Let my mind rest.
Let me eat.
Don't control me,
Leave me,
Let me calm.
Someone help me!
I can't stand it anymore,
The doors close,
The roof falls through.
I'm the worst when I feel the highest,
I'm the highest when I feel the worst.
Worn torn limbs,
Heavy weak legs.
Body's giving up
Cya!
Help me.
There's too many signs,
Red flags,
Aren't they pretty?

Whispering Secrets
When did I become,
Yours?
Tiger, tiger,
When did you run?
Hey, hey
Baby come here,
Follow my finger,
Push down on my neck,
Hum me a lyric.
So, take my Death,
Take my blood,
Drink my soul.
You hear the walls?
The ways they breathe,
Inhale,
Out,
Make it mine.
Whispering,
They speak,
They shout,
Loudly,
Loudly.
Tell me your secretes,
Spill your guts out to me.
I won't tell,
Hum, hum,
Talk, talk,
Did you notice the small child?
The window,
The skit.
Hey there,

Hey there, honey,
Come my way,
See my chest unbuttoned,
Ribs open,
Peer past me.
Hey, hey,
Hey, hey,
Whisper, whisper,
Spit in my ear.
Choke me,
Make me beg,
Breath, breath,
Inhale,
Tell me your secretes.
Whisper, whisper,
Come my way.
Walk past my gaze,
Pitter patter,
Sit down Maryln,
This'll be quick.
I don't want to take much time off,
What a busy woman.
Tell me,
Whispering secrets,
Traveling by car,
Hop on.
Wheels turn,
Turn,
Secretes, secretes,
Cut so deep.
Pitter patter,
Make it mine.

Whisper, whisper,
Hush hush,
Take my soul.
Take me in.

If You Don't Want to Think About It
If you don't want to talk,
Then you don't have to think about it.
You don't gotta talk,
Then you don't gotta talk.
You don't gotta like it,
You don't have to talk.
I wanted,
To be by your side,
I wanted,
To be your stride.
But it's too late,
To follow me now.
It makes,
No sense,
My heart is aching.
If I wanted to make mistakes,
You should've,
Just let me roll it.
If I wanted,
I could just have it.
But I'm still broken,
Fingers are still curling,
Makes no sense.
My pro-frontal lobe is throbbing.
My love is shatter-her-er-er-ing,
Is call-al-al-al-ing.
It's driving me,
Insane,
It's making me,
Question.
It's not really working,

I want to be shaking.
But here I am falling,
There's no telling,
What I am wanting.
If I,
Didn't want think about it,
Then I shouldn't have thought like that,
Like that.

Hunger

Voids,
Spinning danger,
Oh no,
Here we go.
Sit down,
Pull up a chair.
Sit my darling,
Legs spread widely,
This'll be a lot.
Listen closely.
It's okay,
It's fine,
Let's go outside.
How rude,
How mean,
How nude,
What did I see?
My hunger,
Throbbing,
Feed it.
Give me everything,
And more.
I need more.

Spinning danger,
Let's go in it.
I leave,
How fucking rude,
Oops.
Why can't people just shut up?
We won't work,
I ain't comin back,
I've left it all behind.
Come chase me,
If you want me,
Come and get me.
I ain't moving so don't drown.
Hunger,
Feed my burden,
Let me have you.
Burning passion,
Late at night,
I shouldn't think,
Hands running throw my hair,
Names popping up everywhere.
Hunger,
Let me have you.
Hunger,
Wallets,
Ching, ching,
Money, money,
Throw it up to me.
I'll keep it safe,
Leafy green.
How nice it feels,
Touching my skin.

Hunger,
Watch me,
Watching her dance like that,
Up and down,
Side to side,
Ground up,
Come home with me.
Mommy's busy,
Hide the body.
Dish after dish,
Keep it comin.
Lick my fingers clean,
Sticky,
Juicy,
Running down my chin.
Lips plump,
Bring the milk,
Gaping hole.
Bring another plate,
Fill until,
I'm plump,
Like a cheery,
Pluck me from my vines.
Spinning danger,
Hunger,
Hunger,
I'm a wolf, bitch.
Eat you in halves,
Piece by piece,
Till there's blood pooling the forest,
Traces of DNA,
Come back I haven't finished.

Pick your brain apart,
Let me in,
I have to see,
What's operating,
What makes you think.
Ludicrous,
Get the stitches,
Put me to rest,
DNA, DNA, make me say crana, frana, tu, tana.
Punished,
Make me your art.
Creeping,
For you seeing.
Gently running,
To the sink,
Continuous.

A Light Unknown: A1
And the light of dark,
And the light of darkness,
In the light of the store,
In the darkness,
Of the role,
That I'm blind too.
And the things,
That I'd love,
To come upon,
In the latest version,
Of my life that I'd live.
If it was still a choice,
Of mine to take.
Why did you throw it all away?
There was something that was mine,
There was something that I needed,
In this life of darkness,
Without a light.
God dammit,
Why'd I stay, there was nothing in store that I could take.
No,
No,
No,
No,
There's something that makes sense in the laughter that has haunted me, since I stared at the face in the wall.
Fuck it,
Why'd I take,
Why'd I stay on the stairs?
Where there were screams,

**On the walls,
And blood still in the air.
The shit that still stained,
My mind from that day,
That day where the light went away.**
The light of dark.
The light of darkness.
In the light of the store,
In the darkness,
**Of the role,
That I'm blind too.**
Oh, why did it stop,
To see me go,
Across the floor,
across the woods by the door.
Pitiful,
**Slowly leaving his side,
Slowly grabbing the sky.**
Not knowing,
The hand that it dealt,
Was far more,
Scarier than it felt.
It was slippery but I held it up,
Up to my chest, not knowing whose it was…

Falling & Failing: A2
Falling,
Is what I do,
When I'm away from,
Your clasp,
Failing,
Is what I am,
When I am myself.
When in this world,
Is it okay to be me?
Just provide a,
Sweet and simple,
Melody.
For my ears to listen,
And my heart to cry.
I feel like I keep, falling, falling,
Harder when your hurt.
I keep failing,
In keeping you safe,
I keep hurting your precious smile,
I keep failing and falling.
What did I do,
To deserve you?
Why is God publishing me?
Seeing you change,
And die before me,
Because of my mistake.
I know I'm fucked up,
More than you think.
You can call me psychotic,
You can call me dumb,
You can't see the cuts,

Because there deeper than you think.
They're inside me,
They're still bleeding.
And I'm dragging you down with me,
I DONT WANT TOO!
I keep falling, falling,
Harder when you hurt.
I keep failing, failing,
In keeping you safe.
In keeping your precious smile still smiling.
I'm selfish,
I want that smile to fade, for someone else.
I want all of you,
To use,
To enjoy,
For all the wrong reasons.
SO WHY DO YOU KEEP FOLLOWING ME?
When I'm nothing but a failure who keeps falling.
What did I do
To deserve you?
Why is God publishing me?
Seeing you change,
And die before me
Because of my mistake
Because of my goddamn mistake in wanting something for myself.
Just walk away,
While you still have breath to do so
Or else you'll become my hostage,
Screaming to become free.

I'm nothing but a speck of dust flowing like the waves in the night ocean not knowing where I'll go or who'll I'll hit, or kill, or love…

Foolish: A3
How foolish, foolish, foolish of me to have let you in.
How foolish, foolish, foolish of you to have look past my sins.
It was so foolish,
To let go,
To let things in,
Let things,
Go.
Do something you didn't expect of me.
Yes, you're a flower,
Blooming in my mind.
With broken wings,
Down,
Down,
Far away.
Moving,
Running,
Leaping,
Leaving my side.
Her side, his side it's,
Side.
How foolish,
How sad,
Of you to accept me,
And all the scars I come with,
And all the monsters that follow me.
You're a rose petal falling,
Beneath my feet.
A cherry blossom,
Blossoming in the spring.
Slowly being poisoned,

By my touch,
Dying in my arms.
Why did you do it?
Why did you trust me?
Grab my hand,
And hold it close,
To your chest,
Without knowing,
Who's it was,
Who dealt it.
Not knowing what I might do with it,
What I could do to you,
Why did you stay?
By my side,
When I disappeared,
Disappointed you,
I killed you from the inside out.
Yet you still walk,
Still love me,
Still talk to me.
How foolish, foolish, foolish of me to have let you in.
How foolish, foolish, foolish of you to have look past my sins.
How foolish,
How sad,
When I broke you,
When I shattered the,
Light in you.
You're like heaven,
I'm like hell.
I'm scared of being without you, I'm scared of nothing,
I'm scared without a reason…

Scared Without a Reason: A4
I'm scared,
Of the things around me.
Of the things,
That surround you.
I know,
I know,
I know.
I must run,
But sometimes I want to walk.
I want to talk,
I want something in this world,
I want your fair skin,
And faint eyes,
The beauty you behold,
I want something.
I know,
I know,
I know,
You're scared,
Of being you.
You look at the faces in the crowd,
Instead of me,
Instead of the man holding you,
Loving you,
Wanting you.
I just want you safe,
I just want you to see,
The world that I see,
The world around you.
The things you love,
And have a good time.

Holding hands and singing to the sounds,
Of birds tweeting,
In the night sky.
I know,
I know,
I know,
I'm invisible and your blind to see me.
But I'm still here,
I'm touching your heart.
I'm still alive.
I just want something,
To feel,
To love,
To have,
To be wanted.
I know,
I know,
I know,
I must run,
But sometimes I want to walk,
I want to talk,
I want something in this world.
I want your fair skin,
And faint eyes,
The beauty you behold.
I want something,
Want you to know,
That I'm here right now.
I'm not leaving,
You grieve and I smile.
Let's switch roles for once,
Put everything on me,

Be happy.
Be proud,
I'll crawl,
I'll limp,
You run,
Far away.
You keep saying,
You want to stay,
But run goddammit,
Cause you can.
You've got a life to live,
I'm okay,
I'm fine where I am.
Because even if I can't have you,
I have the things around me.
I have the sky,
And the bottom of the ocean,
If I don't have you, I won't die,
And neither will you.
I have the sky,
And the bottom of the ocean.
I have the eyes that hold the truth,
The smile that hurts the most,
The heart that's big enough.
You're small,
Precious,
I own all,
You own none.
And I'm okay.
I'll be fine without your love,
My dear.
I'm letting go now,

of your hand, knowing you'll fall
But you'll heal, because the only thing hurting you,
Is my poison…

Stop: A5

Just fuck off.
Be happy.
Be stupid.
Be a lunatic.
Just don't give a shit,
Cause that's what you are,
Nothing in this world.
Oh, no, you're losing,
Everyone you love.
You keep smoking,
That shit that don't make sense.
You keep,
Dumbing yourself down.
And for what?
To look cool?
Well then just fuck off.
Don't want no family,
Then just leave.
Don't want no love
Then just go.
You keep saying you're getting better,
But you can't stop.
So go somewhere else,
And don't stop,
Don't stop.
Don't make my mind numb,
And feelings fade.
Don't crush my heart,
And go on with your brigade.
Cause your dumb,
And you're not even related to me.

No more,
No more.
Ya, don't give a shit?
Then go to hell.
Just go!
Just fuck off!
Or stop everything you're doing wrong.
Just stop,
Just stop.
Just walk out.
If your hot,
Just drop,
Just drop.
Just,
Dead in the ground.
I mean your wishing it right?
Get the fuck out
Just stop,
Just stop.
Talking about nothing,
About the things,
That no one cares about.
Cause you keep saying,
It over and over,
Like it matters.
Sleep someplace else,
Hurt someone else,
Don't come near me,
For a hug,
With your toxic hands.
"I love you"?
That's just bullshit.

I thought I was nothing,
I thought I was messed up,
That was until I met you,
and that ain't no compliment.

Temptation: A6

You're like a temptation,
Always wanting,
Always giving,
When I don't do anything.
What's this about?
I know you like the chase,
So why stop now?
Let's keep going,
Running from my temptations,
Running,
Running like a cat.
Leaping,
Leaping like a dog.
Let's keep rolling,
On the tracks.
Let's keep playing,
Running away from our temptations.
You're like a temptation
That I'm not giving into yet.
I'm still hungry,
Let's just play,
I ain't starving yet.
So, let's keep running,
Away from the temptations.
It's getting hotter outside,
Until my skin is fried,
It keeps getting colder,
And harder to breath.
I want to run,
Cause I'm scared,
To touch anything.

I'm afraid,
To give you all of me.
I'm not confident,
"I'll hurt you
It's all I do"
That's all,
I think about.
So don't ask questions,
When I run,
Even when I'm exhausted,
Even,
When I can't no more,
It's cause I'm wanting to be held.
To resist.
Because you're the temptation of my life,
The only good one,
Left.
So, let's keep the good times going
Running,
Running like a cat.
Leaping,
Leaping, like a dog.
Let's keep rolling,
On the tracks,
Let's keep playing.
Running away from our temptations.
Running away with smiles on our faces.
I'm not ready yet,
But wait,
Soon I will be.
I'll tell you first.

Want: A7

Is it that bad to want something?
Always being judged,
When I'm whipped for you.
I'm a sucker for the way you look at me.
I'm going crazy when I look at you.
Don't you see?
Why look at the other side?
I'm standing right here,
Looking at you,
Everyday.
You're like a drug,
To my heartache.
I'll do anything for you,
But you can't seem to notice,
I'm whipped and winded,
For a chance.
Holding you,
Touching you,
Kissin you,
Is all I want.
Is it that bad to want something?
Always being judged,
When I'm whipped for you,
I'm a sucker for the way you look at me
I'm going crazy when I look at you
Don't you see?
Please return the heat,
And the want.
Because I'm going crazy,
When you ignore,
When you tease,

When you skip a beat.
I want to see you,
In that suit,
In that dress,
Hair all long,
Covering your shoulders.
Cut short,
All gelled up,
Nails painted,
Or big rings on your,
Fingers.
I'm going crazy when I look at you
Don't you see?
Do you see?
My heart beating when you,
Turn around,
To lock gazes,
To be you.
I'm whipped,
For you,
And all the little things,
You do.
I'm okay,
To keep going.
That game of catch,
Maybe sometimes,
Can we stop,
And let me win,
For once.
I'm whipped,
Head over heels,
Of your scent,

Of your smile.
Just return the love,
Notice how you're driving me crazy.
Pacing around,
Over that look,
On you.
Just notice.
I know you know,
And it's okay to give in,
To the right things,
Time to time.

Dream: A8
You're like a dream,
I keep running to,
Except I can't keep up,
I can't move up,
To you,
You're too,
Too,
Everything I'm not.
You're everything I want to be,
I want to stop running,
But my legs,
Won't stop.
Won't give up.
Nothing's,
Working,
No more,
Nothing goes my way.
I know I wanted to run,
I wanted to fly,
BUT NOT ANYMORE!
I can't take the pressure,
I can't take the sight,
Of being let go,
By you.
I'll survive,
But it will take years.
To heal,
To be whole again,
To be 'okay' again.
I wish you weren't so far away from me,
The distance,

Wasn't so long between us,
Before.
You're like a dream,
I can't conquer.
One that will stay that way,
One that won't come true,
No matter how much I wish,
For it to be real.
You're a dream,
I want so bad,
And I want to hold that hand.
I'm running because you dropped me,
'Do you love me?'
I think and yell,
But you turn your back.
It's a turn off,
You're weak,
What the hell?
Don't you know I'm weaker.
You're my nightmare and my sweetest desire.
Your hair flowing in the wind,
I want to run my fingers through it.
You're my only and every dream.
My camera role filled with our imaginary memories.
Our houses,
Our décor.
Our bed, and shower.
Snuggled up with our towels.
What a dream,
I feel for you.

Lights Out: A9
One normal day,
Running by the train,
And hurting,
With a smile.
The sun blocked,
Out,
And homes left,
Without a sight.
Nothing makes sense.
My ears are ringing,
And my sight has gone out,
Like a flame.
Everything went wayward,
Without,
One warning.
I can't see,
Poor and unfortunate souls,
Crowd,
My fresh body.
I feel pain,
But where from?
I'm hearing screams,
But they feel like my own.
I can't tell.
What's wrong with me?
What happened,
No one's answering,
Everyone's ignoring,
They're all laughing.
People are grabbing at me,
Trying me,

Not acknowledging,
The tears strolling down my face,
And blood shedding.
I'm still a child,
Right?
I haven't grown up yet,
Right?
I have an innocence, still left in me,
Right?
Wrong.
I'm feeling lost,
Even though,
I feel you,
Standing near me,
Trying to talk to me.
Noise is being blocked out,
Like I'm listening to music.
Except with silence.
No one can match my height,
Cause no ones in my sight.
I'm feeling trapped in my own bed.
I'm strapped down,
In my head.
My arm tied up,
Around my body.
I can't move them,
I can't smile,
At them,
At the flowers sitting beside me.
With padded walls,
And never-ending calls.
Nights with darkness around,

My body,
Doesn't feel right.
My eyes all puffy,
And head still spinning.
I keep wondering,
I'm a child still,
Right?
I haven't grown up yet,
Right?
I have an innocence, still left in me,
Right?
Wrong
I mean,
I feel like a kid,
Right?
I haven't grown up yet,
Right?
I have an innocence,
Buried with in me,
Right?
Buried beneath me,
Right?
Answer me!
Just answer me,
You always talk, so talk to me.
What's the problem now?
I'm losing all my sanity.
I'm still okay,
Right?
I haven't died yet,
Right?
I'm still caring,

Right?
IM STILL HUMAN,
RIGHT?
Wrong
Otherwise, you wouldn't be in here.
Tied up, strapped down, like a useless slug.
All broken down, with eyes that don't work,
And ears that fill with radios.
Do you sincerely think,
YOU ARE, OKAY?

New Chapters Begin Fast: B1
Sitting alone,
In a solemn room.
My hands tied back,
Staring at the wall,
With eyes looking,
For a snack.
There's nothing staring back.
There's nothing looking forward.
With padded walls,
And secluded sound,
Is living even worth it?
There's no getting out of it.
Why am I sitting here?
No life in the way I breathe,
No huff,
In the way I move.
The days and nights mix in together.
The walls keep moving,
Back and forward.
What's the point,
In trying to stay hopeful?
What's the point,
In trying to keep the sanity?
What's the point,
Of trying to save me?
When you're the reason I'm in here.
New chapters always begin the fastest.
They always want the light,
Always want the win,
But what if I give it to them?
New chapters always start the new game.

They always come the same way.
Always at the weirdest times.
My wine glass is empty,
So, what?
My throat is unhealthy,
And?
My cuts are now bleeding,
Onto the floor,
Keep going.
I'm wanting to get out,
...
Won't you let me????
Stop fucking complaining.
New chapters always like to start,
When you aren't looking,
When your wings have broken,
And the sky has fallen.
A time when everything seems right,
Only to become wrong.
A new day, new day,
Will come shining, shining,
Twined with the moon,
Darkness.
A new soul, new soul,
Will come cheerful, cheerful,
And come in hopping, hopping,
Not knowing,
What might happen.
New chapters always begin the fastest,
They always want the light,
Always want the win,
But what if I give it to them?

New chapters always start the new game,
They always come the same way,
Always at the weirdest times.
By now you've noticed,
A new chapter is beginning,
The middle of the story is coming.
A new chapter having trouble with ending.

Help: B2
I can't seem to help you,
My friends.
I can't seem to leave you,
My sorrow.
I keep thinking,
How I could have helped you.
You can get it,
If you really want it,
If you really need it,
If you're really hurting,
If you look hard enough.
Running hard enough,
Getting out fast enough.
Unlocking the chains one by one.
I always feel as if I can't help you.
I can't make you smile,
When you're sad,
And I mean nothing to you,
Even though I am.
Even when you tell me,
"I love you."
I ask you,
Is it possible for me to make you happy?
Do I please you enough?
Does the dopamine run through you,
When you're with me?
You reply,
"You can never make me fully happy,
But little moments with you
Make me delighted."
What am I supposed to say to that?

Should I be happy?
That I can't help you,
Achieve the full amount of happiness,
That you desire.
Should I feel okay,
Knowing that you don't,
Feel good during the time you're with me.
If I can't help you,
Then please,
Don't hesitate,
To rid of me.
To find someone to help you,
Find the glow,
That's within you.
Find the lost child,
Inside you.
If I slow you down,
Then leave me.
If you lie to say,
"I love you"
Then don't waste your breath,
Run me over,
Leave me behind.
Make your pain stop,
With someone else's help.
If I'm not doing anything,
Then find someone,
Something else.
Just walk away,
I'm not going anywhere,
Anyways.
Since I'm trapped,

Here,
Locked in here,
Unable to leave,
Because you've already left me.
**I'm stuck here staring at the wall again,
Talking to myself telling you to leave, when you're already gone,
Regretting letting you go,
Not helping you successfully,
Yet you ruined me.**

Left Unseen: B3
I already explained it,
I already told you it isn't possible,
Monsters don't get to go out in the light.
Left unseen,
Left unnoticed,
Until he backs,
Into the truck,
With a million knives,
Starting to duck.
Left unheard,
Left by me,
Causing her,
To see you bleed.
A river of,
Blue water,
Coming by from the green tears,
That stain your fingers.
Oh, your fingerprints,
Stamp my body,
From head to toe,
Crevasse to ear.
Left unoriginal,
Left untouched,
In a sitting chair,
Looking,
Glancing,
At the ground.
What makes you smile?
What makes you feel?
What makes you think?
What makes you want?

I don't understand it,
The way you run,
The way you scurry,
When your hurt.
The way the right people,
Get squashed,
Like bugs,
Beneath a building.
The way the glass shatters,
It's like music to my ears.
The way it scores,
The reality,
Shattering.
Left unseen,
Left unwanted,
Left in the room,
Unfed,
And undaunted.
What's that behind you?
What's that beneath you?
The childhood leftovers,
The one you never wasted.
Then what am I?
Left unseen,
Left,
Left,
Left,
Never right.
Always wrong,
Always in the shadows,
Of the pink tree,
In the open field.

On a train,
Whose tracks.
I played on.
Left,
Wrong,
Left,
Wrong,
Never, never,
Right.
Never, never,
Wasted,
Be the best,
You can be,
Don't mess up.
Don't make mistakes.
Be normal,
Be like her,
Don't get good grades,
Get good guys.
You mistake!
I never wanted you!
You belong in the left ,
You belong unseen,
You belong on the tracks,
So, it's easier to get rid of you.
Left,
Left,
Left, always left unseen.
I'm the thought in the back of your head,
Every smile you bear,
Every person you meet.
Slowly,

Painfully reminding you,
I was left unseen by you.
It's okay I'll forgive you,
For leaving me and making me regret,
It's okay,
It's okay,
Let me console you,
Let me do to you what happened to me
Left unloved, and with no sanity.

Winter: B4
Spring is so warm,
A warmth I want.
With a breeze in my hair,
Happy to be alone,
To be with me,
But I'm stuck in the saunter,
I'm stuck in the winter.
Snow falling from the windows,
The ceilings filled with,
Not fluffy, white, waters
But hard ice,
And breathtaking bites.
Spring is so nice,
Something I want so much,
Something when,
I close my eyes,
I try to remember,
But the feeling,
I can't,
Seem to taste.
Walking outside,
No coat,
Taking it in,
Every breaking,
Frozen breath.
Titling my head to the sky,
Watching the frozen bits,
Fall on my skin,
Becoming pale.
A day in spring,
Please I need it,

It's so cold.
In the winter.
I'm stuck in the winter,
I can't feel the summer.
I long for the feeling of getting out in the sun.
But I can't seem to remember,
What it looks like.
A day on the tracks,
Back when life was good,
Back when it made sense,
Back when they visited me.
I see you looking out,
The train window,
Hoping to see me,
Spinning around in the sun.
A pink tree in a field,
Where they went,
All the men.
I want that,
I want to be seen with them.
Enjoying the youth,
I'm stuck not using.
Just a day in the spring,
With those people,
On a nice warm day.
My skin is breaking,
Like glass.
If I remember the spring,
The nice leaf filled trees,
Instead of the branches,
Yet unseen.
Everything falling down on me,

Without a reason.
I can't even cry,
Without the tears freezing.
I hate to admit it,
I'm stuck in the winter,
I can't feel the summer.
I long for the feeling of getting out in the sun,
But I can't seem to remember,
What it looks like.
I wanted so much more,
For myself.
I wanted to meet,
Those idols,
Out on that burlesque,
Beautiful blue day,
With eyes,
With suns in them,
That one **spring day**.
I want to swim in the sand and play in the ocean,
I want to pluck several flowers to place behind their ears,
But all I can do is imagine from afar,
And hope one day,
I'll get out of here.

12 Little Lies: B5
One look is all it took,
To make you fall harder than you ever wished for.

One day,
One night,
One day,
One cry.
It only took one,
Night,
For all the little lies.
12, 12, 12,
Is knocking on your door,
12, 12 men,
One of them is dead,
But his body's never found.
11, 10, 9,
Two of them are burned,
1 is of them is slaughtered.
But one body's never found.
8, 8, 7,
One was a woman,
6, 6, 5,
One of them have drowned,
The rest were never found.
4, 4, 3,
Minutes is all it took,
One pulled the trigger,
One took the sewer.
2, 2, 2,
One of them is scarred.
Now where is the other one?
1, 1, 1,

Where are the lies?
12 was never found, yet never was he gone.
12, 12 men,
If one of them is missing,
Did he even ever exist?
11, 10, 9,
Two of them are burned,
So, their bodies don't exist,
But what happened to the other one?
1 of them is slaughtered,
But the body never found.
How is it that that's true?
8, 8, 7,
One was a woman,
But where is the other one?
6, 6, 5,
One of them is drowned,
Yet the nest was never found.
4, 4, 3,
Where the hell did 3 go?
2, 2, 2,
One of them is scared,
1, 1, 1,
Explain I'm getting bored.
12 never made it,
11 is alive,
7 isn't real,
5 never died,
3 went home,
And number 2 is still traumatized,
Number 1 went to you.
Killed them for the fun.

Number 1 is still alive,
Fighting all alone,
Looking in the mirror,
One of them is me.

Fear: B6
I don't want to be afraid anymore,
It's not worth it.
I want to feel the waterfalls in my stomach, And the
butterflies in my heart.
I want a flower to blossom in my mind,
To blow me away.
I want the sun to shine on me,
And everything around me.
Illuminating the things I never noticed,
The little things,
The way I love,
The way he likes,
And the way she smiles,
I want to love them all.
I don't want the fear,
Please take it from me.
Unchain these chains,
And let me feel the light.
I want a happy ending as well.
Why won't you give me one?
I want something to do,
Give me something to fondle with.
Give me bunny ears,
And pick me up by my feet.
Give me rosy cheeks,
And short hair.
I want something too.
Let me twirl in the sun,
Alive and well,
Don't keep me hidden.
I don't like it.

Let the sun burn my skin,
And fill my eyes.
Give me feet to walk on,
And arms to swim with.
Give me a gum wrapper ring,
And a flower crown.
I don't want the fear,
Please take it from me.
Unchain these chains,
And let me feel right.
I only need 3 years to know,
I will Marry you.
I want to be your something.
I want to be the one,
To make you so smile that brightly.
Just give me 3 minutes,
Hold your hand,
Kiss those lips.
Lay my head down on your lap and sleep.
Please make me,
Your little doll,
You can carry around.
I've broken myself down,
Just so you can come,
Like a princess,
Like Prince Charming,
To put me back together.
We aren't that bleak,
I know how you feel.
I can see it in your heart,
It radiates off you.
So, give in,

And come get me.
Cause I'm waiting,
I'm,
Not,
Going,
Anywhere.
Please I'm still sitting here,
In winter.
And so, cool me down
So, my breath doesn't come out,
And all I can feel is warmth.

Sorry (Sorta): B7
Please I'm still sitting here,
In winter.
And so, heat me up,
So, my breath doesn't come out
And all I can feel is warmth.
I just want to feel the life that,
Lives in you to know,
It's okay.
Let me take a moment,
To say I'm sorry.
I sorta,
Didn't know how to feel,
What to do,
I just want,
To stop saying that.
Every time I open up my mouth,
I don't want to say,
"I just wish I wanted"
Let me just have.
I'm sorry,
Sorta.
I'm sorta,
Regretting everything,
That happened.
All I wanted,
Was to hurt,
So, I could feel something,
Cause sometimes I can't feel nothing,
At all.
I'm sorta,
Weak without you.

An answer,
Is all I crave.
Give in to my craving.
I hate to be cliché,
But you make me,
And I make me.
So,
Let me take a moment,
To say I'm sorry.
I sorta,
Didn't it know how to feel,
What to do,
I just want,
To stop saying that.
I wish I could get you,
Out of my mind,
But days come and I can't,
Seem to remember the scent of the air without you.
Days like today,
You take over my mind,
And mess me up.
Until I see you,
Walking up to me,
Arms open,
And smile on you.
Until I feel a heart that doesn't beat,
Until you come to wake me.

Half Moon: B8
Half of me is gone,
In Hiding,
And only you can see,
The me that illuminates.
The way I want it to be seen.
I won't be hiding anymore,
So, prepare
For the real thing,
For all of me,
If you let me,
Only if you let me.
Half-moons,
Halfway through,
Almost there,
We stop.
Got a long way to go,
Across the other half,
Across the dark floor.
The lights gone,
Bring your flashlights,
And another soul.
Another brain,
Cause I swear one thing too,
Typist gonna loose something to write,
History gonna loose something to study,
Student gonna loose the school,
Your gonna loose the soul in you.
So, prepare.
There's one way,
Around the moon we go.
We can take a rocket,

Or a plane,
Depends on where you go.
On a perfect night,
Let's make out way over there,
On the moon.
Hallways here,
Rooms there,
Teachers in the back,
Not replanting.
I won't try hiding anymore,
Not any longer,
No more should I feel this way.
Like I'm a terrible person and people mean nothing.
You're something,
You're something,
To me.
I'm sitting outside,
The stall door,
Crawling,
Tailing behind you,
Just look back.
Look around,
You're hiding too.
My heart's for you.
It aches when seeing you.
It's driving me insane.
It's making me so plain.
It's adding more color and taking less out,
If you don't want something,
If you don't want me,
Then say it,
Say it right in my eyes,

So, I can get it through my skull.
When I'm with you,
Nothing makes sense,
I feel like,
Skipping two steps,
Three steps,
Four,
How much farther will you go?
Let's take a trip to the half-moon in the sky.
Let's take a rocket ship and soar through the sky.
Let's say 'Hi' to the stars,
And bye to the worries.
I won't be hiding anymore,
I won't be hiding,
So, prepare,
For the real thing,
For all of me,
If you let me,
Only if you let me.
Please let me.

Manipulation: B9
It's a funny little thing,
Playing with ones feeling.
Playing with someone,
To drive them crazy.
Oh, it's a funny little thing,
When that person become you,
And touches the middle walls,
That your stuck in.
Twisting the walls,
And only eating the cream off the Oreo.
Preaching anything,
Mad,
Waiting,
For a miracle to disappear.
It's a funny little thing, emotions,
They can change so easily.
Hate being yelled at.
I hate being hated.
Don't tell me I did good.
Don't tell me I did bad.
Words will always hurt me more than they hurt you,
Cause they stay in my head.
Stuck in my mind,
In the back of my throat,
Of my head and another weight on my shoulders.
Manipulation,
Manifestation,
All funny things,
I love to play with.
Tease,
Make into my mind.

Debugging the last bit of me,
Drugging me against my will,
Till you find me in the morning,
Against the trash bag you threw out.
I didn't want to end up like this,
I had so much planned.
I wanted to fly a plane,
And meet you on the moon.
Look past the sun,
Holding you in my arms.
I hate seeing you hurt,
But I love seeing you wander,
Wander right into me,
Like its fate.
Wander into my open arms,
Like it's meant to be.
So many things thrown out,
Cause I didn't trust you,
So many things that didn't begin.
A persona meaning nothing.
Not a glimpse of light,
Not a glimpse of hope,
Nothing ever goes right.
When I'm there,
I'm banging the side of my head,
With a fist made with my hand.
Please don't follow,
Please don't smile,
When I'm here,
Get lost.
Don't loathe around,
And put down the racks,

By the stairs for me to take.
So many personas,
That didn't get to bloom,
To many things in my mind,
Left there,
Because you weren't here,
To set them free.
They've became rotten,
And started to mold,
Beneath my feet.
Manipulation,
Manifestation,
All funny things,
I love to play with,
Tease,
Take into my mind.
Debugging the last bit of me,
Drugging me against my will,
Till you find me in the morning,
Against the trash bag you threw out.
I'm rolling on the floor,
Clinching myself,
Clutching my stomach.
Throwing up,
The innocence,
The life from my lungs,
Play some music for me,
Fore enter,
Forevermore.
Play 'Man in the Mirror'
As I lay in my coffin.
To remind me of the further I could have gone.

The future I could have had,
The persona,
The people,
The person I left behind,
Because I chose to be insane instead of seeing you leave.
Manipulation,
Is so fun when it's with yourself.
When it's with me, when no one's looking.
When they all left.
One way or another we will all be left there lying against the trash bag of evidence you left,
That reeks, for me to find.
I know what you did and why I'm here. Would you like me to tell the others?

The Evidence: B10
Can't you just see me?
Can't you just be satisfied with me?
Fuck it.
I don't even mind it anymore,
The blade slicing my skin,
The skin on my arms peeling.
I'm dealing with this world,
The heart break.
So many things,
Left undone because you decided,
To find the evidence.
That bag reeks,
It's filled with blood,
What's for dinner,
Meat,
Who's?
Yours.
I don't even mind anymore,
I am the evidence of your sick experiments,
The tubes down my throat,
The abuse you called love,
The heroine in my tears,
The stops,
I yelled for.
Honestly, I don't even care anymore.
It's all for the pleasure.
Your eyes are,
The one who belong in this jacket,
Strapped against my body.
I WANT OUT!
Someone save me.

I was never crazy.
My chair won't move forward.
Help me.
I can see you sitting there,
Preparing my medication,
That I don't need.
Frying my entire mind,
This is just for your own sick pleasure,
Having me tied up so I won't move,
So, you can continue to abuse.

If I die, then no one will be your test subject.
I ask for bigger doses,
And more pills fill my system.
You're getting your wish,
I'm slowly killing myself,
With your medicine.
I was fine before I ran into you,
Before I became your subject.
You used me for my blood,
My body,
My mind,
So, you can conduct on me,
Now you've even labeled me crazy.
I'm the evidence to your testing,
You used my love against me.
Driving me mad with that smile,
Give me a stronger dose,
I don't even mind anymore,
I'm so bored,
And the drugs love me.
The feeling is so nice,

Blades in my mouth,
I can't get them out.
You want to know what happened?
Get me a new doctor.
I'm as pale as one of your ghosts.
I'm shaved down to my bones.
I don't even mind anymore,
I am the evidence of your sick experiments,
The tubes down my throat.
The abuse you called love.
The heroine in my tears.
The stops,
I yelled for,
Honestly, I don't even care anymore,
It's all pleasure.
So pleasurable the I.V pipes,
I'm so bored,
Put in more.
The tolerance keeps going up,
Stop it,
Do what you want with me?
It's driving me insane.
I need something to do,
Let me do something.
My new doctors come to visit me

My Toy: C1
"I'm your my new doctor."
<u>Don't confuse yourself, you're just the new toy.</u>
<u>My toy.</u>
<u>My toy.</u>
My toy is so plain,
She doesn't play with me,
She just stares at me,
Asking questions.
<u>"I want to play,</u>
<u>I'm bored."</u>
She doesn't listen.
<u>My toy,</u>
Has curves,
She's cute in those glasses.
<u>"I like the hair down"</u>
She puts in up.
<u>My toy,</u>
Doesn't listen,
I can't punish her,
Unless she gets closer,
But she's scared to touch me.
<u>"I don't bite."</u>
She moves away.
<u>"You're no fun."</u>
"How can I be more fun?"
<u>"Come closer."</u>
<u>My toys'</u>
Lips are so soft,
She so fragile when she sits,
Her hands feel so nice,
When they glide against my jacket.

<u>My toy,</u>
Is so scared,
To be near me,
But she can't resist,
The urge,
Of placing her lips on mine,
Puckering them up,
When I ask.
Obedient,
How adorable,
<u>My toys'</u>
So weird,
She looks at me,
With eyes that I've forgotten how to read.
She wears different colors that hurt my eyes,
She's not dull and likes the cocky type.
<u>My toy,</u>
Likes to speak and continues,
To ask questions.
She's falling,
As I'm faking so much,
She's unchaining me,
Just a little more.
She likes the intimate,
She unlocks slow,
Because she's desperate for the touch,
I'll give her,
Without telling her the cost.
She's **<u>my toy</u>** after all.
Nothing more,
She's nothing more,
I remind myself.

Don't be crazy,
She's almost,
There.
She's almost,
Handed those keys in your mouth,
Just keep going what you do.
My toy.
My toy.
My toy.
She's making my head hurt,
I need to get out.
I can't stop myself,
She keeps aiming my mind,
She keeps smiling,
Playing games.
My toys'
Weird,
She keeps using,
She keeps crying,
I keep feeling,
STOP IT!
JUST STOP!
My toy,
Your eyes are stuck in my head,
They took my toy away,
They won't give her back,
My toys' gone,
And now I can't play.
She was nice,
She was pretty,
They took her away.
I hope,

<u>She's okay.</u>
<u>I miss her lips touching mine.</u>
<u>She was a strange one,</u>
<u>But she tried,</u>
<u>Tried harder than the others.</u>
<u>I couldn't use her,</u>
<u>She was,</u>
<u>To much,</u>
<u>Too kind,</u>
<u>To innocent.</u>
<u>I liked my toy,</u>
<u>I want her back.</u>

Stories: C2

You want a story,
I'll give you one.
Once lived a man,
Alone and cold.
Scared was she,
She roamed the train track,
Every day until he met,
A someone.
Mysterious,
Was he,
Happy was she.
They played together,
Everyday.
Made plans for the future,
Lifted his feet,
And spun her around,
Held onto her,
And kissed his lips.
Until he got an idea,
Testing, testing,
Are the tubes working?
Is the blood coming?
Is the bed rising?
Are the chemicals working?
"You're doing great."
Tie the straps harder,
Loosen them too.
Let me breathe.
What's that?
What are you doing with my body?
I feel numb,

The medicine feels so nice,
Give me more.
Drug me more,
Have me more,
I can't control the way I speak.
I can't speak.
The bruises are deeper,
Bring the knife,
Yank it from my hands,
As I rip my jeans.
My stomach feels so weird,
Mind If I open it up,
And see it?
Pump me full of blood.
Bliss in my mind,
And blood on my hands.
Did I do that?
I don't know.
I never noticed.
I can't feel anything.
Gliding, glowing,
Across my arm,
I can't feel it,
Do it more.
Keep going,
Nothing's working.
Try again.
Trail and tribulations,
Grin and fire,
A bed without me.
Within the meaning,
A house of horror.

As I walked right in.
Sitting in a chair with electricity,
Roaming around my bones,
Shattering my arms,
Breaking my chest.
I'm on the ground,
Unable to breathe.
<u>"I'm not done yet,</u>
<u>Where's my pleasure?"</u>
Throw me out,
In the middle of the night.
With my blood,
Across the floor,
I go,
Call the cops.
Lock me up,
I'm wearing a jacket,
Find my doctor.
What is it you want to study with me?
<u>"Everything."</u>
I hate this.
Washing away the senses,
With doses,
And pills.
Give me more,
I like it too much.
I want out too much.
This is the way,
Do what you wanted.
Drug me,
For your explanations,
For your expectations.

Experimenting,
Rats poison in my lungs.
Keep taking,
Keep going,
It's only making me feel better,
And worse.
By washing me away,
I love being a pet of your experiments.
I'm food to your curious brain,
I'll make the expiration date,
Don't worry it's soon,
I'll begin to eat the bones you behold.
If I don't get out,
Let's go on a walk together.
What stopping you?

Faking It: C3

I give up.

I can't trust you.

Don't ask me anymore.

Don't talk,

Don't be,

Don't make.

It makes my mind,

Hurt.

The way everything,

Twirls.

The way everything seems to stare,

At the open walls,

And the closed,

Shattered,

Broken windows.

Of the town halls.

Hall there,

Square here,

Chalkboard,

Mantled over,

Sides and locked,

Down to the tiniest person.

Make good of yourself.

Don't leave alone to myself.

Boredom,

Ennui,

Apathy,

Uninterested,

Nothing of those is something I like to own.

I just love faking it,

Haunting in the presence of love,

And making good,

You believe you mean.

Giving up on the real shit,

I like the fake,

The cocky,

The stupid,

They're easy to control.

I just love faking it.

The feeling you long for,

To make you seem full.

Weariness,

Languor,

Accidie,

It fills my lungs and shoots,

My chest,

The ribs,

The ribs,

Save the ribs from cracking,

Piercing the inside of my heart.

Does it even matter?

Sense,

Mind,

Likelihood,

Love.

Nothing,

Nothing,

I feel,

I think.

Empathy?

That goes to the weak.

Crying?

Don't remember.

Summer,

Burn my skin,

To a crisp.

I just love faking it,

Halting in the presence of love,

And making good,

You believe you're alive.

Giving up on the real shit.

I like the fake,

The weak,

The mistreated,

They're easy to align with.

I just love faking it,

The feeling you absolutely despise,

To make you regret,

And want so much more.

Sluggishness,

Malaise,

World-weakness.

Lack of enthusiasm,

Lack of interest,

Lack of concern.

Unconcerned,

It's what I've become.

There's no changing the subject,

The waters keeps on rising.

She keeps on writing.

Breathe keeps freezing,

Limbs start drowning.

The nothing strategy,

Makes sense.

The loneliness,

Starts to crawl,

Up my chest.

Through my skull,

The misery,

it's to miss.

Faking it,

Seems fun,

Seems Duffy,

And diffused.

Singing in the rain,

Without an explanation,

Umbrella and the sand beneath my feet,

Wear white for me.

"I want a bigger dose; they don't seem to be working for me..."

<u>"Okay...</u>

Trust: C4

It's something I've given up on,

Every time I see them pass by.

I've waited here,

For so long,

In the little park,

With the cherry blossoms,

And perfect proposal spot.

One by one they go,

Crying of tears,

Happiness in them,

I see them and feel numb.

I'm numb and deaf as far as I know.

I can't resist the temptation,

And tension,

You bring.

So solemnly,

So shamelessly,

Forget the wine,

Bring the whiskey,

Get me something stronger.

I'm tired.

So tired.

I'm all weak.

The tolerance,

Keeps getting higher,

Keeps holding on tighter.

It's annoying,

It's obnoxious,

How much I want but can't get my hands on.

The trust you called,

Was fake and you knew it.

You knew it was fake,

The snake,

And smiles,

The bites and bike.

Riding, tailing,

Trailing, stocking,

Bring back,

Trust,

You don't know the meaning.

You abuse everything I gave you,

I never wanted this to happen,

Not to me,

Not to you.

You sacrifice so little,

It sickens me.

Spent my life trying to debunk the heart you own.

The story you hide,

It's caused me to lose mine.

I'm walking alone,

To a watering hole filled with sand,

That I already knew about,

You affect me in all the bad ways,

And that's what makes it so addicting.

My heart feels so shattered.

My heart feels so dumb,

For trusting someone like you,

Would only look at me,

Would only kiss me,

Would only be with me.

My heart aches as I move farther away.

I can't even remember,

Or tell you the way it hurts,

Because it's all about jealousy.

Why do I feel so jealous?

How long am I going to feel this way?

I don't even love you.

Nothings The Same: C5

I'm walking up the stairs,

Repeatedly,

All day,

All the nights,

That don't exist.

Never ending,

I don't know where the hell I'm going.

No one's going to try and stop me.

Nothing's the same.

The cool breeze,

Passing by my shoulders.

Nothing's the same.

The way the buildings lean,

And look at me.

Nothing's the same,

Never will be.

The way the wind feels,

It's not okay,

It's not human.

The way they stare,

The judgment roaring in my ears.

Every little whisper,

Every little thing,

Ever little comment,

The cement is swirling,

The air is twirling,

Wrapping itself around my neck,

So, I can't ever breathe.

Never,

Ever,

Never,

Till the tether,

Seems to break.

On my way back,

Back to that hell that I miss.

Something doesn't feel right,

In every breath I take,

In every word I speak.

I'm losing all my strength,

The dominance running away from me.

I'm getting weaker,

By the day.

Damn the tides are closing in,

I can't even stay,

Because there's nothing,

In my way.

I'm so tired,

Being tied up,

Being completely bored.

Inviting death to eat my soul.

My heart keeps thumping,

When I look at your sick smile.

The smile that I despise,

But I can't even hate.

It all keeps beating,

Harder when you reach out.

Touch my hand again,

Graze over me with,

Your hands.

I want to let go,

But I can't no more,

Not after I've begun,

To want you again.

Nothing's the same.

The cool breeze,

Passing by my shoulders.

Nothing's the same.

The way the buildings lean,

And look at me.

Nothing's the same,

Never will be.

Nothing will ever be,

Nothing will ever seem,

Nothing can ever stop,

And be the same thing.

Hurry: C6

You keep hurting me,

And you know.

You don't do anything about it,

And keep pushing me.

Keep pushing all the buttons I don't want you to.

For the first time in a while,

I want to cry,

I want to drop dead,

Beside you,

It's breaking me apart and you don't care.

Come and hurry back before I break.

Before I won't talk anymore,

Before the tears fall.

Hurry,

Please.

I need someone,

I need love.

Putting my hood up,

Blocking it all out.

Walking down those cement stairs,

Take me on a bus,

That leads to a graveyard.

I feel so distant.

I feel so tired,

And weak.

Help me,

Find peace,

In my head,

In my heart that's aching and acting up around you.

Hurry before I fall.

Before I go.

Before I hide.

Protect me.

Make me feel needed.

I need someone who will hold me,

You aren't that person.

I'm letting go for real this time,

I can't love you.

I've come to terms, and I can't hold back anymore.

I won't interfere.

I can't hurt you.

I need you,
For every breath.
Even just for a minute,
Even just for a moment.

H.I.F.R: C7

It's just H. I. F. R,

Happiness In a Fake Reality.

When in someone who's killing me,

Loving me,

Only me.

I don't understand why I hate you so much.

But hate colors from undesired love.

Tell me the truth,

Tell them the truth,

It wasn't me but you,

You're fighting with yourself.

I'm no man,

No woman,

I'm a conscience.

I'm trying to help,

You drugged yourself.

You did this yourself.

I didn't intend to hurt you.

I'm-

I can't make you happy.

I can't hold your hand.

Stop fighting with one another.

Stop biting each other,

But we can't.

We can't let go,

From the dreams,

That live in us.

So, we stay and smile,

Through the misery I've put up with.

I'm abused and loved.

I'm happy and sad.

Lonely and sweet.

Used and treated well.

Smashed with a beer bottle,

And glued back together.

It's just H. I. F. R,

I feel nothing when I'm around you.

I surpass everything I do,

I never loved the work,

And things I hate.

The things I claim I need,

I don't need,

They betray.

They call it love but how?

If he can't feel, how does he know?

It's just H. I. F. R

I don't need anything else,

Just don't leave me alone.

I can't take it anymore,

My story is too long,

I hate this feeling.

They want to save me, but I must save them first,

It's a sacrifice I don't know how to make.

Sacrifices: C8

I'll sacrifice it all just tell me the truth.

I did it,

It's me,

I did it all.

The little story I made up,

To save my soul.

I put them in danger.

It's life,

It's like that,

It's the best I'll get.

The 7 it's my life,

I have to help them,

Or they'll die.

I've got to get up,

I'll sacrifice it all just tell me the truth.

I'll save all the souls I hurt,

I'll make it all better,

I'm better than the devil's hands.

I save it all in one go.

I don't know why,

That dying doesn't scare me,

But living does.

I'm not okay,

I don't know what to feel anymore,

Please need me and hurry towards my way.

I'm ready,

I'm scared of life anyways,

Buts it's okay to die sometimes.

Save her life,

Save him from the mysteries of the knife.

I'll sacrifice it all,

Just tell us the truth.

Don't keep me waiting,

And until you do,

I'll make a plan,

To save this man.

I can't make this by myself,

But I started it with a target on myself.

I sacrifice my life,

My little,

Undesirable life,

That I worked so hard to keep,

But it's okay,

Nowadays I don't feel pain.

You can stab me with a knife,

"Did it hurt?"

Not really.

I'll give up everything,

Just take this pain away.

My mind needs to trust my body and take my pain away.

Resolve it,

Dissolve it in water and pour it onto a plant.

I'll sacrifice it all, just tell me the truth,

I started it didn't I?

I created this world, didn't I?

I hurt myself, didn't I?

I did this to save myself didn't I?

Yes.

I'm going to die, aren't I?

Yes

Stories End Too: C9

Stories like mine end too,

Stories without happy ending,

With me in the ground.

In this life I love 7,

And found love for the 8th.

She said she loved me,

My toy left.

He said he'd heal me,

He wasn't real.

I was fidgeting with me,

Fighting with only me.

I was the devil who's hand I held,

I was the one who loved the hatred self of mine.

I did this.

Stories like mine end too,

With bad endings and happy people,

I can hear the cries of sadness but it's okay.

I sacrifices the love I had for you.

7 people,

With an 8 lost and hurt.

It took a moment in time to realize I did the wrong.

8 people confidently move the lands,

Hand in hand,

One in the ground.

Stories end too,

Some mad,

Some sad,

Some happy,

Some terrified.

It's all okay,

I made it okay,

It's just a story,

Nothing more,

Just a dumb book,

Started by a 13-year-old,

Looking for a home.

It took years,

But it happened,

The home is with the 7.

7 men, and 7 family members she'll hold close to her chest.

1-Knowledge

2-Tutelary

3-Anguish

4-Fatuous

5-Tumult

6-Quaint

7-Euphoria

8-R.E.D.

We are all Repulsive and Eloquent, with Demons within us.

www.ingramcontent.com/pod-product-compliance
Lightning Source LLC
LaVergne TN
LVHW012025060526
838201LV00061B/4468